DANCE AWAY

by **George Shannon**

illustrated by **Jose Aruego**
and **Ariane Dewey**

MULBERRY BOOKS • New York

Library of Congress Cataloging in Publication Data
Shannon, George.   Dance away
For children aged 4-8.
Summary: Rabbit's dancing saves his friends from becoming Fox's supper.   [1. Rabbits—Fiction.
2. Foxes—Fiction. 3. Dancing—Fiction]
I. Aruego, Jose, ill. II. Dewey, Ariane, ill. III. Title.
PZ7.S5287Dan [E]   81-6391
ISBN 0-688-10483-5
AACR2

To Ava

    –J.A. and A.D.

To Ray Turner, a friend most dear

    –G.S.

Rabbit loved to dance.

He danced in the morning. He danced at noon.
He danced at night with the stars and the moon.

Every time he danced, he smiled a big smile.
Everywhere he danced, he sang his dancing song:

    left two three kick right two three kick

    left skip right skip

    turn around ...

When he saw his friends, he would begin to dance with them.

    left two three kick right two three kick

    left skip right skip

    turn around...

His friends liked to dance, but not all the time.

Still, every time Rabbit met them, he would make them start to dance.

    left two three kick right two three kick

    left skip right skip

    turn around!

Rabbit's friends began to hide when they saw him coming.
"Watch out!" they would call, "here he comes again,"
 as Rabbit danced by singing:
    left two three kick right two three kick
    left skip right skip
    turn around!

But one afternoon when Rabbit danced toward his friends,
no one moved. No one went to hide.
Rabbit called, "Hello," but no one said a word.

As Rabbit got closer, he knew the reason why.
They were trapped by Fox. Caught for his supper.
"Good," growled Fox as Rabbit came near.
"Another for dessert!"

Now all of them were trapped. They knew they could not
all safely run away.
Most sat and shivered as Fox began to choose which rabbit
would be first.
But Rabbit asked, "Please," as he nodded to the others,
"could I dance with my friends just one more time?"
Before Fox could answer, Rabbit took a friend's hand
and began to sing his song. Then each took another's
and they all began to dance.

 left two three kick right two three kick
 left skip right skip
 turn around!

Fox was so surprised he did not know what to do.

But when Rabbit danced by, he told Fox what to do.

"Dance!" Rabbit said and they grabbed his legs.

left two three kick right two three kick

left skip right skip

turn around!

Fox screamed "Stop!" but the dance went on.

   left two three kick right two three kick

   left skip right skip

   turn around!

Rabbit kept singing and they all kept dancing.

Every step they took, they danced a little faster.

   left two three kick right two three kick

   left skip right skip

   turn around

   left two three kick right two three kick

   left skip right skip

   turn around!

As they came to the river, Rabbit sang with a shout:
  left two three kick right two three kick
  left skip right skip
  TURN AND JUMP!

Everyone jumped, but halfway across the river
they let go of Fox!
He crashed splat splash into the cold river water
as Rabbit and his friends landed safely on the grass.

Then before Fox had time to swim back to land,
Rabbit and his friends danced home as fast as
they could go:
    left two three kick right two three kick
    left skip right skip

turn around home!